The Kings' Castle

"Claude!" moaned the other ghost, appearing through the wall.

"Go away," ordered Annabelle. "You're frightening Claude."

"No, I'm not," said the other ghost. "We're having fun, like we always used to."

"He- -e-e-lp!" quavered Claude, and went to hide under Annabelle's bed.

"What do you mean?" said Annabelle. "Look - he's scared stiff."

Claude lay under the bed, as stiff as a knitting needle.

Dare you *another* Young Hippo Spooky?

The Screaming Demon Ghostie
Jean Chapman

Scarem's House
Malcolm Yorke

Four Young Hippo Magic stories to enjoy:

My Friend's a Gris-Quok!
Malorie Blackman

The Little Pet Dragon
Philippa Gregory

Broomstick Services
Ann Jungman

The Marmalade Pony
Linda Newbery

The Wishing Horse
Malcolm Yorke

Laugh with a Young Hippo Funny!

Bod's Mum's Knickers
Peter Beere

Emily H and the Enormous Tarantula
Emily H and the Stranger in the Castle
Kara May

A NN R UFFELL

The Kings' Castle

Illustrated by Philip Hopman

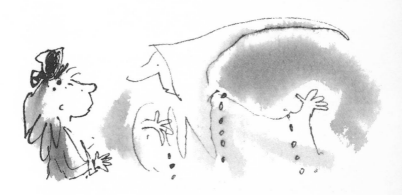

To Amy and Adrian

Scholastic Children's Books,
7–9 Pratt Street, London NW1 0AE, UK
a division of Scholastic Publications Ltd
London ~ New York ~ Toronto ~ Sydney ~ Auckland

Published in the UK by Scholastic Publications Ltd, 1995

Text copyright © Ann Ruffell, 1995
Illustrations copyright © Philip Hopman, 1995

ISBN 0 590 13175 3

Typeset by Contour Typesetters, Southall, London
Printed by Cox & Wyman Ltd, Reading, Berks

10 9 8 7 6 5 4 3 2 1

The rights of Ann Ruffell and Philip Hopman to be identified respectively as
the author and illustrator of this work have been asserted by them in
accordance with the Copyright, Designs and Patents Act, 1988.

The Wandering Knight

Claude was a ghost. He lived behind a wardrobe in a very old castle, the sort that has battlements and dungeons.

Mr and Mrs King and their daughter Annabelle lived in the castle too. They looked after it and showed visitors round, especially on Bank Holidays and weekends.

The visitors liked Claude best. Not many

old castles have real ghosts that haunt the battlements and dungeons.

Sometimes he howled horribly in the middle of the night. Sometimes he appeared suddenly behind Mr King in the mirror. This was usually just as Mr King was about to shave. Sometimes, for a change, he would scream suddenly from behind his wardrobe when the Kings were showing people round.

He had haunted the castle for almost three hundred years. This made him quite historic. Mr and Mrs King and little Annabelle warned friends who came to stay that he screamed in the middle of the night. If they knew, they wouldn't be too frightened.

The best time was at Hallowe'en, when Mrs King strung buns on strings and Mr King put apples into a bath of water for bobbing. Annabelle made lanterns out of pumpkins and invited all her friends to a party.

"You've met them all before," she told Claude. "You can frighten them if you like. They won't mind."

Claude rattled his chains happily.

"Can I bring some friends?" he asked. "We could have a really good haunt, as it's Hallowe'en."

Annabelle said he could, and so Claude invited all his friends too.

A castle is a very good place for a
Hallowe'en party. It is full of long, gloomy
corridors where you expect ghosts to pop out
at you even if they don't. There are stone
floors which make lovely echoey footsteps.

Claude and his friends enjoyed themselves
very much. They jumped out at one of
Annabelle's friends just as he had his teeth
nearly into an apple. He fell flat on his face
into the bath of water.

They screeched suddenly just as another friend had the stickiest bun swinging in just the right direction. She was ready to take a really big bite, but the scream made her move her head. The bun swiped her on the nose instead.

They moved the lanterns and candles so that the castle was full of flickering shadows. Nobody knew which was a shadow and which was a real ghost. Even the ghosts weren't sure.

Claude's friend the Wandering Knight especially wasn't sure. He was the sort of ghost who carries his head under his arm. He had only put his head down for a second so that he could find his handkerchief, and then he lost it.

It is difficult to see when you haven't a head. The rest of his body wandered round the castle. It wandered through doors. It wandered through walls. It didn't know where it was going. Annabelle had to take the Wandering Knight by the hand and make him sit down.

"*We'll* look for your head," she said. "Just stay there."

But of course you can't hear if you haven't a head. The Wandering Knight didn't know he had to sit still, and wouldn't know until his head was found for him.

Claude's friends kept bumping into him in dark corners.

"He's lost his head!" they laughed in their thin voices.

Annabelle simply couldn't find the head. She went back to ask the Wandering Knight if he could remember where he had put it down.

The Wandering Knight wasn't there any more. He was wandering along a dark corridor. Mr King met him on his way to the kitchen.

"Have you gone off your head?" asked Mr King. But the Wandering Knight couldn't hear so he didn't answer.

Annabelle collected up her friends. She sent some this way, some that. Some she sent upstairs to the battlements. Some she sent downstairs to the dungeons.

She sent a friendly ghost with everyone to keep them safe.

They searched everywhere, three times over. But nobody found the Wandering Knight's head.

They found the Wandering Knight several times. He was still wandering because he didn't know he was supposed to sit and wait for the head to be found.

Finally Annabelle went to Claude. "Does his head speak?" she asked.

"I think it laughs," said Claude.

But they hadn't heard a head laughing by itself anywhere.

It was nearly midnight. It was time for everyone to go home from the party. Annabelle's friends waited for their parents to come and collect them. Claude's friends remembered there was another party in the graveyard at midnight.

But the Wandering Knight couldn't remember anything. His head was still missing.

As Annabelle and her parents waved goodbye to the last guest, they heard a strange noise in the castle.

"Be quiet, Claude," yawned Mr King. "If you want to go on haunting, go to the graveyard party."

But it wasn't Claude.

It was someone laughing.

"The Wandering Knight's head!" cried Annabelle. "Listen!"

Through the walls of the hall wandered the Wandering Knight. His head was still not under his arm, but the sound of laughing came with him.

"Where's the party?" said the Wandering Knight's voice. "I seem to have lost my way somewhere."

Annabelle suddenly had an idea. The

Wandering Knight's suit was very baggy, with large pockets in his jacket. One of them looked very bulgy.

"Look in your pocket!" Annabelle told him.

The Wandering Knight fished in the bulgy part of his jacket. There was his head, laughing like a lunatic. "Now I remember,"

said the Knight. "All those flickering lights were making my head spin. I wanted to mop its brow with my handkerchief. I must have tucked it into my pocket with the handkerchief afterwards. It was dark in there, but I had a really good sleep. I'm all ready for a good haunting party now."

But even Claude had had enough of hauntings for one night. They sent the Wandering Knight down to the graveyard, where he kept his head firmly under his arm for the rest of the night.

2

The Haunted Ghost

It was after this Hallowe'en party that something very strange happened to Claude.

He had gone for his usual walk along the top corridor. He wasn't rattling his chains as much as usual because he was rather tired. It had been a very good party. He stopped outside Annabelle's attic door for a little rest.

But the sound of dragging chains went on.

Claude turned to tell his chains to be quiet.

They were lying quite still in a pale misty heap, right beside him.

And the sound of dragging chains went on.

Claude faded himself into Annabelle's bedroom door so that he was only a faint glimmer shining on the brown paint.

But the sound of dragging chains went on, slowly, down the corridor. They went on past Annabelle's door, and on and on, right to the top of the staircase.

Claude couldn't see anything at all, only his own chains lying quietly and peacefully by his side.

He was petrified!

Annabelle half woke and saw Claude shaking in the door.

"It was a nice party, wasn't it?" she said drowsily. "I did like your friends." She turned over and went back to sleep again.

Of course, thought Claude. It's only one of my friends having a joke. He oozed out of the door and shouted, "This is *my* chain-dragging corridor. Go home. The party's over."

There was no reply, but the sound of rattling chains began to come back along the corridor again. Claude was so terrified that he disappeared right back through Annabelle's door and out of the wall on the other side.

From inside the castle came a long and frightful wail, and the chains went on dragging and clanging up and down all the staircases.

It was an awful night! Claude tried to creep back into the castle without being noticed, but whenever he appeared, the sound of chains and dreadful moaning followed him.

He crept into Mr and Mrs King's bedroom. He pretended he was a curtain on the four-poster bed. They were floaty, white net curtains. Claude looked just like another floaty, white net curtain. Then, just as he felt safe, the curtain on the other side of the bed began to move about in a draught. Then it billowed out like a sail. Then a howling gale nearly ripped the curtain from the bedpost.

Mr King woke in a bad temper.

"Claude! If you can't behave I'll send you to haunt that nasty bungalow at the bottom of the hill. That'll cramp your style a bit!"

Claude shivered into the bathroom.

"Boo!" shouted a face, grinning at him from the mirror.

Claude screeched back into Annabelle's bedroom and shook like a pale green, wobbly jelly on the lampshade.

Annabelle woke up properly this time and scolded him.

"Be quiet, Claude. If you want to go on haunting, go to the graveyard party."

"It's n-n-n-not m-m-m-my f-f-f-f-fault..."

But as he tried to explain, he saw the other ghost beginning to appear through Annabelle's skylight window. A terrible cry rang round the castle.

It was impossible for Claude to escape. The quicker he disappeared and reappeared somewhere else, the quicker the other ghost followed him. He hid in one of the taps in the kitchen, but the other ghost ran out with the cold water and made weird whirls in the sink. He wound himself round the strings of the grand piano, but the other ghost played a haunting melody on him. He slid between the pages of a book in the library, but the other ghost found a shady story and began to read it in a high, shrill voice.

By this time the whole household was awake. Mr King stalked the ghosts with a fly spray because he thought it might quieten them down. Mrs King floated about in a long white dressing-gown, wringing her hands. Mr King mistook her for one of the ghosts and sprayed her with fly spray. Annabelle put her pillow over her head but it didn't keep out the dreadful cries in the castle.

Claude shivered so much that he looked like a television screen gone wrong, and his teeth chattered like teacups. He went back to Annabelle's bedroom and tried to hide inside her pillow.

"I'll never haunt anyone again," he moaned into her ear.

"What *is* the matter, Claude?" said Annabelle, quite cross. "You don't usually behave like this after a party."

"Claude!" moaned the other ghost, appearing through the wall.

"Go away," ordered Annabelle. "You're frightening Claude."

"No, I'm not," said the other ghost. "We're having fun, like we always used to."

"He-e-e-e-lp!" quavered Claude, and went to hide under Annabelle's bed.

"What do you mean?" said Annabelle. "Look – he's scared stiff."

Claude lay under the bed, as stiff as a knitting needle.

"He can't possibly be scared. I'm his brother," explained the other ghost. "We used to have great fun, haunting together."

"My brother?" said Claude, and appeared right through the middle of Annabelle's bedclothes. "I haven't seen you for two hundred years."

"They pulled down the house I was haunting, so I thought I'd come and live with you," explained the other ghost.

And so he did.

But Mr King insisted that the brothers took it in turns to haunt the corridors. "Or nobody will ever get any sleep," he said.

He made an exception for Hallowe'en nights, of course, when Claude and his brother made the castle the spookiest place in the world.

3

Claude's Present

One hot Sunday afternoon, when the castle was quiet and even Claude had gone to sleep in the cupboard under the stairs, a witch came along.

Claude's brother was asleep too. He was dangling like a gargoyle at the side of the castle. He woke up with a watery shiver when the witch screeched into his ear.

"Hey, stop it," he said. "Screeching's my job."

"Never mind that," said the witch. "Listen, it's your brother's anniversary on Thursday. Give him this."

She handed over a sack. An ordinary, brown sack. The sort of sack you might get seed potatoes in.

"What anniversary?" asked Claude's brother.

"He's been here three hundred years. On Thursday," said the witch.

"What's inside it?" he asked.

"Never you mind," said the witch. But she couldn't help whispering something into his ear.

"What?" said Claude's brother, but the witch refused to repeat what she had said. Instead, she flew off on her broomstick, cackling, "If you tell anyone what I've said you'll be turned to stone!"

"I think she said if I tell him I shall be turned to stone," he said to the ravens in the West Tower.

They cawed with laughter, which made Claude's brother cross. "I'll turn *you* to stone if you're not careful," he threatened.

He took the sack and gave it to Claude.

"Don't open it till midnight on Thursday," said Claude's brother.

"Which midnight?" asked Claude. "Before Thursday or after Thursday?"

"At the end of Thursday," said his brother.

Claude looked at the sack. It was just an ordinary, brown sack. The sort of sack you might get seed potatoes in.

"What is it?" asked Claude. "Is it skulls, is it worms, is it *bones*?"

"I'm not telling you," said his brother. He didn't like to tell Claude he hadn't heard what the witch said.

"Have a look," said Claude.

"I can't do that," said his brother. "In any case, if I tell you I shall be turned to stone."

"Might keep you quiet for a bit," said Claude unkindly. He went off in a huff to moan round a few dusty corners.

All through Monday Claude kept taking a look at his anniversary present. It was fat. It was knobbly. It was just the sort of shape for a really interesting present. He poked it with a wispy finger. Something wriggled inside, he was sure.

He went to Annabelle.

"Have a look inside," he said. "Is it bats, is it belfries, is it *bones*?"

"I'm not going to look," said Annabelle. Claude's brother had had a word with her. "In any case, if I told you what was in there I'd be turned to stone."

"Just tell me who's going to turn you into stone," said Claude indignantly. "I'll sort them out. I'll scare them to bits."

And he went off to practise scaring people to bits at the village school. He practised so hard that Mr King had a letter from the Headmaster the next day, asking him to keep Claude away. The children couldn't concentrate on their arithmetic, he said.

On Tuesday Claude went to Mr King.

"Please have a look and see what's in my present," Claude asked Mr King. "Is it ghouls, is it ghosts, is it *bones*? Tell me!"

"I can't do that," said Mr King. Claude's brother had had a word with him. "In any case, if I told you what was in there I'd be turned to stone."

"That wouldn't do you any harm," muttered Claude. He bounced at a slug and frightened it so much that it told all its friends to leave the castle grounds at once. It was a pity Mr King didn't know this. He would have given Claude a medal.

On Wednesday Claude went to Mrs King.

"Will *you* look inside my present?" Claude said to Mrs King. "Is it screams, is it howls, is it *bones?*"

"I can't do that," said Mrs King. Claude's brother had had a word with her. "In any case, if I looked and told you, I'd be turned to stone."

"You'd make a nice statue," said Claude

kindly. But it gave him a good idea.

Around the castle were quite a lot of statues. A statue is made of stone. If a statue told him what was in his present, it wouldn't matter.

Claude howled down the Great Hall, "What's in my present?"

But the statues were made of stone and did not answer.

He tried outside. There were some modern statues made of plastic out there. Perhaps they'd like to be turned into stone.

"What's in my present?" he screeched.

But the statues were made of plastic and could not go and look. There was nothing for it. He would have to wait until Thursday night.

All through Thursday he waited. He waited in the attics and spun ghostly yarns with a whole lot of spiders. He waited along the top corridor, dragging his chains backwards and forwards like a hundred ships weighing anchor. He went outside to haunt the huntsmen and howled with their hounds.

On Thursday night the witch came back. She knew what was inside his present all right.

But her plan had gone wrong.

She thought all the family would look inside Claude's present and tell him what was in it. Then they'd all be turned into stone.

She had hated the family ever since Mr King said she couldn't come to his Hallowe'en party last year. So she was going to get her own back by turning everyone into statues.

Mind you, if she hadn't said that they'd all be turned into stone, they might have looked. It was a bit silly of her really.

So she was rather cross when she saw everyone sleeping in their beds, all warm and wriggly. Nobody had turned into a statue. Not even Claude's brother.

Claude hung on a turret, waiting for midnight to strike. He had his sack in his ghostly hand.

The witch cackled a nasty witch-like laugh and did a three-point turn round the tower.

"I bet you don't know what's in there!" she shrieked.

"Tell me," said Claude. "I can't wait another minute."

There was only another minute to go. The hands of the clock creaked slowly round on their rusty wheels.

The witch couldn't wait another minute either.

"You're going to look really stupid!" she said. Her screams of laughter frightened Claude's favourite bat colony in the turret. The bats all came out in a cloud and covered the moonlight. Just as she hovered right at the top of the turret stairs she yelled, "You silly ghoul, it's NOTHING!"

Well – that witch had no brains at all, because in a trice she turned to stone. Good, grey, hard stone.

The broomstick clattered all the way down the stone staircase. The stone witch went SCRUNCH on to the floor of the turret, wobbled a bit, and stayed there.

"Well, what a cheat," said Claude. "After all that waiting."

When the clock struck midnight he opened the sack, just in case, but it was true. The knobbles and wriggles were just bits of nothing.

He dropped the sack over the stone witch and went off to help the owls haunt the dark wood.

A year later, Mr King went to the turret to do some clearing up. He picked up an old sack and found the statue of a witch.

He poked it with his finger. The stone crumbled away and blew into the air like dust.

The witch had turned into nothing, just like her present.

Pipes

There was trouble with pipes at the castle.

When it rained, water ran down the outside of the pipes. It spilled over the top of the gutters. It gurgled down the drains in all the wrong places.

Mr King called in the plumbers.

The plumbers came with plungers to suck out the drains. They came with scrapers to scrape out the gutters. They came with long rods to push down pipes.

Annabelle went outside to look.

Claude and his brother went outside to look as well. Annabelle told them to stay hidden.

"We don't want to scare them," she said. "And don't make any noises."

"Not even a small moan?" said Claude.

"Not even a short shriek?" said his brother. He was disappointed. He liked frightening people.

"Not even a small moan or a short shriek," said Annabelle.

Claude found a place to hide. It was a newly cleaned pipe. His brother found another place to hide. It was a newly cleaned gutter.

Every time the plumbers cleaned a pipe or a gutter, Claude and his brother moved. They watched the plumbers at work all day.

"There's a lot of smoke around," said one
of the plumbers to Annabelle. "Have you got
a blocked chimney too?"

"It's only the ghosts," said Annabelle.

The plumber laughed. He didn't believe
her. He thought that the ghosts in a haunted
castle were fake ones, like at the fair.

"You've got a good smoke machine, I must
say," he said.

Annabelle looked for the ghosts. She needed one of them to haunt the Great Hall. The visitors paid their money to see ghosts, and were very disappointed if Claude or his brother never turned up.

"I'm sorry. They're outside today," Annabelle told the visitors.

The visitors looked outside, but only saw little wisps of smoke.

"It's all a fake," they grumbled.

Annabelle was cross with Claude and his brother. "You're supposed to be helping me," she said.

"You said we mustn't frighten them," said Claude. "I'll just watch them clean this pipe. I'll come in a minute."

"Or a century," said his brother.

But neither of them went into the castle to haunt the Great Hall for the visitors. Instead they followed the plumbers round all day.

At night the ghosts decided to have a really good haunt outside the castle. They needed to make up for not frightening the plumbers all day. All the pipes and gutters and drains were clean and empty. Everything sounded twice as loud in there. They shrieked in the down pipes. They moaned in the drains. They dragged their chains all over the gutters. It sounded as if there were fifty ghosts in the castle.

Up and down the castle, drainpipes were streaks of spooky light. The ghosts were playing tag inside the pipes.

Claude gave a specially good scream outside the Kings' bedroom window, and his brother rattled both sets of chains along the gutter. Mr and Mrs King woke up.

"They might have done that this morning," said Mr King crossly. "Five visitors asked for their money back today."

The two ghosts made a bloodcurdling gurgle in the drains. It was so loud that Annabelle woke up.

54

"Not now, Claude," she said crossly. "I wanted you to help me this afternoon but you never did. Go to sleep now."

It was a good idea. They were both tired with all that watching during the day. They were even more tired with all that screaming in the pipes. They were too tired to do their usual haunting.

"You can have my turn to haunt the top corridor," said Claude.

"That's all right. I'm too sleepy," said his brother.

So neither of them haunted the top corridor.

Claude thought it would be very comfortable to sleep in a drainpipe. His brother decided to sleep in the gutter.

In the night it rained.

Claude didn't like the feel of water dribbling down him. His brother didn't like the feel of water sloshing past him. All that swishy water kept waking them up.

Claude tucked himself in with a few wodges of old leaves. His brother found a couple of last year's birds' nests to cover himself up.

Water ran down the outside of the pipe outside Mr and Mrs King's bedroom. It was blocked up by Claude's warm leaves.

Water spilled over the top of the gutter outside Annabelle's attic bedroom. This was blocked up by Claude's brother's nests.

In the morning they woke up, threw away the nests and leaves, and began doing their proper jobs. Claude rattled his chains along the top corridor, practising his moans. His brother jumped out at little girls and boys from behind the wardrobe.

Mr King sent for the plumbers again.

"I can't understand it," said one of them. "I did that gutter first. I remember the curly bit at the end."

"I know I did that pipe," said the other plumber. "It's the one with the squiggly bit at the top."

Mr King said they had to do it again for nothing.

They were even more puzzled when they saw the pipe and gutter were quite clean. Even so, they spent hours doing another very special cleaning job on everything.

Claude and his brother watched.

"Serve them right for not believing in us," said Claude in his thin voice.

Claude's brother thought they should be shown about ghosts. He slid up the drainpipe from the bottom. The first plumber was at the top of his ladder. The ghost popped out of the top of the pipe and yelled, "BOO!"

The man had such a shock that he slid all the way down his ladder and bumped his bottom on the grass.

"It's a g-g-g-g-ghost!" he cried.

"Don't be silly," said the other plumber. "It's all a fake. You said so."

Claude shot up from the drain by the kitchen door and waggled his pale fingers at the plumber's mate. "BOO!" he yelled.

The other plumber shook like a jelly. He was too frightened even to speak.

Both of them ran as fast as they could, away from the castle. They went so fast they left their tools and ladder behind.

Mr King had to send those back later because the plumbers were too scared to come and get them.

And they always believed in ghosts after that.

5

Annabelle's Birthday

It was Annabelle's birthday. Mr and Mrs King were going to take her to a magic show.

Claude's brother was going away for a few nights.

"I feel like a really good haunt where there are lots of people," he said. "A football ground, or a pop concert. I like to hear lots of screaming."

He didn't take Claude with him. Annabelle thought that was rather unfair. Claude ought to have a treat too.

"Claude would love to come with us," Annabelle said to her father.

But Mr King was cross with Claude. The ghost had put on an extra special haunt for Annabelle's birthday. He waited until it was just light. As the first birds began to sing, he gave a lovely long, loud wail. It echoed over the battlements. It rang round the belfry. It wound round the corridors. Then it died away in lots of splendid shuddering sobs.

"I'm not taking that ghost," said Mr King. A haunting at first light was far too early for him.

Annabelle took her largest purse with her to the magic show.

"Can you fold up very small?" she whispered to Claude.

Claude folded up very small. He just

managed to fit in Annabelle's purse.

The theatre was full. Mr and Mrs King and Annabelle took their seats right in the front row. The band was a bit further down, in the pit.

Claude felt rather squashed in the purse. He oozed out of it and hung in a pale glow by Annabelle's right hand. He could just see the stage.

The magician on the stage made a rabbit appear out of a hat. All the audience clapped. Claude glimmered happily.

The person next to Annabelle poked her in the ribs. "Please put your torch out," he said. "I can't see properly."

Claude had to squash himself back into the purse. He was very bored in there. There wasn't much fun in coming to a magic show if you couldn't see anything.

He sneaked a look out. The person next to Annabelle was looking at the stage. Everybody's eyes were on the stage. Very carefully, he slid out of the purse and crawled along the floor like a smear of spilled ice-cream.

The magician was doing some difficult card tricks. Claude thought they were a bit boring. He could see what the magician was doing with the cards. It might be a good idea to shuffle them up.

The magician couldn't understand it. None of his card tricks went right. Every time he wriggled his hands to make the cards go where he wanted them to, Claude poked a long ghostly finger on to the stage and made them change places.

At first the audience thought things were going wrong. The poor magician became very flustered. Then the audience saw Claude's pale finger reach out from the orchestra pit. The magician was doing it on purpose! They laughed and clapped.

Claude bowed at the same time as the magician.

He was .'t used to orchestra pits. When he sat down again after his bow he fell into the drum kit.

The drummer was doing a special roll for the magician to bow to. Claude was chased by the sticks all over the drum skin. Then the drummer whacked his cymbals together and Claude's head buzzed like one of Mrs King's worst headaches.

The audience thought this was very funny. They clapped like anything. The magician thought they were clapping him. He bowed very low again.

"Claude, don't be naughty!" cried Annabelle. "Come back!"

But Claude was beginning to enjoy himself. He wove himself through the strings of the violins and frightened them into horrible squawks. He switched on the keyboard by mistake. Half of Claude's scream went sharply up. Then it went flat down.

The magician on the stage glared at the keyboard player. He thought he was playing the music wrong on purpose.

It was time for his extra special magic tricks. He always did these when he felt nervous. But that wasn't a good idea – not with Claude helping him!

He pulled strings of birds out of his mouth. Claude fluttered out with the last one and frightened the birds so much that all their feathers flew into the audience.

He did a trick with balls under cups. Claude kept moving the balls when he wasn't looking. Then he juggled with them, all

round the magician's head. The audience cheered loudly. The magician thought he must be mixing up his tricks. He wished he'd brought his book of instructions.

He tried a trick with pieces of string. Claude rolled himself up like a piece of string and tied himself to one of the real pieces. When it was supposed to be tied up, Claude untied it. When it was supposed to be untied, Claude tied it up. The poor magician thought he had forgotten everything.

He decided to saw a lady in half. Claude came out of the two halves of the box in lots of bits. When the magician put the box together again, Claude went together in all the wrong places.

Annabelle began to feel sorry for the magician, even though the audience liked the tricks going wrong.

Then the magician asked if a child from the audience would like to help him. Annabelle got there first. She had to stop Claude somehow.

The magician had a special magic trick with hoops. He told Annabelle to watch when he shook them. They all linked up together. She couldn't see how he did it. He shook them again, and they came apart.

He gave the hoops to Annabelle. "You try," he said. He smiled, because he knew she would not be able to do it.

Annabelle shook them. She didn't know what she had to do to link them together. But Claude had been watching. He knew how it was done. As Annabelle shook the hoops they all linked up together. She shook them again and they came apart.

"What a clever little girl," said the magician crossly.

Annabelle gave Claude a special Look when she came down from the stage. Claude thought it would be a good idea to get back inside the purse.

"I thought I told you not to bring that ghost," said Mr King, when they were going home.

Annabelle just smiled. The magician had been a lot better when Claude helped him.

6

A New Ghost

It was late one Saturday. All the visitors had gone home. There was nothing left of them but a heap of picnic rubbish.

Mr King went round the grounds grumbling. "As if we didn't put out enough litter bins!" he said.

He was so tired that when a ghost jumped out at him he didn't notice it wasn't Claude or his brother.

"Oh, go away, Claude," he said. "The visitors have all gone. You don't have to do any more haunting. Go and sweep up if you want to be useful."

He was only joking, but the ghost took up a brush and began to sweep the path. Mr King was too tired to wonder how a ghost could pick up a brush.

Annabelle and Mrs King had been cooking for the tea room all morning. They had served the visitors with cakes and buns and cups of tea all afternoon. Annabelle went to bed but Mr and Mrs King would have to wash up all evening.

"Can I help?" said the ghost.

"Yes, please," said Mrs King. She was so tired she didn't notice it was not Claude or his brother. She was too tired to think about a ghost washing up.

"Thank you, Claude. Or is it . . .?" She was too tired even to finish her sentence.

The Kings went to bed. They didn't hear Claude dragging his chains along the top corridor. They didn't hear Claude's brother chasing his chains up and down the drainpipes.

They didn't hear the new ghost try out an unearthly wail.

Claude heard it. So did his brother.

They went out to meet the new ghost. It would be nice to have someone different to haunt with.

"What do you do best?" asked Claude. "I've got some lovely chains if you want to have a go with them."

"I like making people scream a lot," said his brother. "I can give you a few tips if you like."

"Yes, please," said the new ghost to both of them.

Claude took the new ghost to the top corridor and lent him his chains.

Well, you should have seen the bother that new ghost got into with Claude's chains! They should have hung on him in a green fog, and made a lovely rattling noise when he walked. But the new ghost didn't seem to know how to put them on. When he tried to wrap them round his legs like knitting they fell on to the floor. The chains helped as much as they could, but the new ghost's fingers seemed to slip every time. In the end the chains just gave up and drooped in a grey mist round his feet.

"That's funny. They don't usually do that," said Claude.

"I'm a very new ghost," explained the new ghost. "I'll soon learn how to do it."

"Never mind," said Claude's brother. "Let's go and make people scream a lot. I usually jump out at them first."

The new ghost was quite good at jumping out of the spare room wardrobe. He practised wriggling his fingers and making a frightening face when he jumped.

"That's not bad," said Claude's brother. "Come with me. We'll find some people to practise on."

Claude's brother oozed through the wall of the spare room. The new ghost opened the door and walked through.

"Why did you do that?" asked Claude's brother. "It's much quicker going straight through the wall."

"I'm a very new ghost," explained the new ghost. "I haven't got my proper body yet. It takes time."

"I suppose it does," said Claude's brother. "I don't remember."

Claude and his brother had to wait several times for the new ghost. He couldn't float downstairs. He couldn't go through doors and walls.

"I'm sure I didn't take all that time to be a proper ghost," whispered Claude.

"He should be able to squeeze just a *little* bit of himself through a wall," Claude's brother whispered back.

The new ghost found a lovely echo in the kitchen chimney. He moaned into the huge fireplace and the moan went all the way up to the top of the castle.

"That's very good," said Claude admiringly.

"Let's all moan all the way up," said Claude's brother. He grabbed the new ghost's arm and began to rise up the chimney like flickering smoke.

The new ghost gave a splendid scream.

"That's even better," said Claude.

"O-o-o-o-o-o-ow-w-w!" screeched the new ghost.

"Wonderful!" said Claude's brother. "Now make yourself thin here because the chimney pot's rather small."

But the new ghost was stuck. Only his head popped out of the pot. His hair was black and spiky from the soot.

"Just shrink," Claude's brother told him.

"I c-c-c-c-can't!" shrieked the new ghost.

Claude couldn't get past, because the new ghost's feet were in the way. He faded through the chimney bricks and came out on to the roof.

"What's the matter?" he said to the new ghost's head.

"I'm s-s-s-s-scared!" moaned the new ghost.

"You've got it wrong," said Claude. "You're supposed to scare other people, not get scared yourself."

But the new ghost's eyes were shut tight and his teeth chattered like a loose skull. "B-b-b-but I'm not . . ." shivered the new ghost.

Claude wasn't listening. There was a car driving up to the castle door.

The ghosts weren't allowed to frighten people until Mr King said they could. Visitors were all right. They expected it. This car couldn't be a visitor, not at this time of night. It stopped very determinedly outside the big wooden door.

Claude and his brother swooshed down and hid in the drainpipes.

"Come on!" cried Claude in a thin, high voice. "Hide!"

"He-e-e-elp!" screeched the new ghost.

Someone got out of the car and banged on the big wooden door. Then they rang the clanging front door bell.

The new ghost yelled from the chimney pot.

With all that noise Annabelle woke up. She went downstairs to open the front door.

"Is my boy here?" asked the lady at the front door.

"He-e-e-ere!" wailed the new ghost from the chimney pot.

"It's only our ghosts," explained Annabelle. "They're not really frightening. And I'm afraid we haven't got your boy. The castle is all locked up for the night."

"He-e-e-ere!" moaned the new ghost's voice down the kitchen chimney.

"I can hear him," said the lady. She walked into the kitchen. Only his voice was there, echoing in the fireplace.

Annabelle went outside. She called to Claude and his brother. They poked their heads out of the tops of their pipes like gargoyles.

"Who is moaning?" she asked.

"It's our new ghost," explained Claude. "But he's stuck in the chimney."

Annabelle looked up. "Don't be silly," she said. "That's not a ghost. That's a boy."

It took Mr King three hours to get the new ghost out of the chimney. The lady wasn't very pleased. Nor was Mr King.

But the boy smiled through his soot as his mother dragged him home. "I had a great night," he said. "Let me know when you give haunting lessons again. I promise not to get stuck in the chimney next time!"

7

The Invisible Ghost

Claude's cousin came to stay.

"You won't even notice he's here," said Claude. "He's always invisible."

"That's a relief," said Mr King. Claude and his brother had been jumping out at visitors and frightening them more than usual. Some of the visitors had even complained.

"He's very musical," said Claude's

brother.

Mr King thought that their cousin might not be such a good guest after all.

"What sort of music?" he asked.

"He likes sitting on the piano," explained Claude's brother.

"That sounds quite quiet," said Mr King. "Your cousin can stay as long as he likes."

He went away to sort out the castle treasures for a special exhibition.

When Mr King had gone, Claude said, "You didn't tell him about the song."

Annabelle came by with a duster. "What song?" she asked, dusting Claude and his brother too.

"He plays 'Happy Birthday to You' on the piano," said Claude. "But only when it's somebody's birthday."

"I've had my birthday," said Annabelle sadly. She thought it would be lovely to have a ghost playing 'Happy Birthday to You' when you woke up on your birthday morning. By the time her birthday came round again Claude's cousin would have gone away. Everybody else's birthday was a long way away too.

"We'll ask him to stay again when it's your next birthday," said Claude's brother kindly.

"How will the visitors know we've got another ghost?" asked Mrs King. It was her turn to sell the tickets today. She liked to tell the visitors which ghosts were in residence.

"If somebody has a birthday he'll play to them," said Claude.

"Don't tell anyone," said Annabelle. "It will be a nice surprise for them."

"And then we can give them an extra cake in the tea shop," said Mrs King.

It was time for them all to help set up the exhibition. There was armour which the old knights used to wear. There were swords which they used to fight with. There were jewels that their ladies used to wear.

Mr King oiled the armour so that it didn't squeak. He polished the helmets and the swords. Annabelle washed the jewels so that they sparkled. Mrs King arranged it all in a

glass case next to the piano.

Nobody saw Claude's cousin on the piano, because he was invisible.

There were double the number of visitors, because of the exhibition. Mr King and Annabelle had to make some extra cakes.

Claude's cousin watched them all as they walked by his piano, but nobody had a birthday for him to play "Happy Birthday to You".

One of the visitors was a burglar. He walked round and round the glass case. He thought he knew how he could get inside it.

Then he went round outside to find out
how he could get into the castle when it was
all locked up.

He wasn't frightened of ghosts, not even at
night.

Claude's brother swooped down from the
battlements and howled in his ear, but the
burglar didn't even jump. The ghost was
cross, and went away to frighten somebody's
granny in the kitchen.

Claude screeched suddenly from the wine barrels in the dungeon. The burglar laughed. He waggled his hands right through Claude's middle. This gave the ghost such a tummy ache that he had to go and hang from the highest drainpipe to recover.

Claude's cousin lay on the piano and watched. He couldn't jump out at the burglar because he was invisible. He didn't make a noise because it wasn't anybody's birthday.

They were glad when the burglar went away.

But the burglar came back that night. He crept in through the dungeons and made his way through to the kitchen.

Claude's brother woke up and gave a spine-fizzling scream.

Mr King woke up and said crossly, "You know I hate being woken up in the middle of the night! Save your screams for the visitors tomorrow."

The burglar wasn't frightened of ghosts. He just smiled.

Claude slid down the drainpipe very fast. He popped up through the wastepipe in the sink and howled horribly.

Mrs King woke up and moaned, "Be quiet, Claude! I've got one of my headaches."

The burglar smiled again, and began to climb the stairs.

The ghosts whizzed round Annabelle's bed, wailing and groaning as hard as they could. But Annabelle just slept on.

Just as the burglar reached the glass case, all the clocks in the castle struck midnight.

And suddenly the piano began to play "Happy Birthday to You".

Annabelle woke up. "But it isn't anybody's birthday!" she cried.

She ran to wake her parents. "Somebody's in the castle," she said. "Claude's cousin is playing the piano and it isn't anybody's birthday!"

Mr King woke up and said crossly, "Who's playing the piano at this time of night? I'll give them what for!" He ran to find a poker.

Mrs King decided to have her headache later. "Where are those ghosts?" she asked. "They're supposed to be our burglar alarm."

They found the burglar, still standing by the glass case.

He burst into tears. "How did that piano know it was my birthday?" he wailed.

He wasn't afraid of ghosts, but he was very frightened of pianos that played by themselves!

8

The Skeleton in the Dungeon

The Bank Holiday was cold, wet and windy. Not many visitors came to the castle. Mr King didn't need Annabelle to help in the kitchen. Mrs King didn't need Annabelle to help sell tickets.

The ghosts felt wet and windy too. Claude went to play with the water falling in twists down the drainpipes. He found it difficult to get back up from the drain because of the grating. He had to make himself very thin to get through the holes. Once he forgot to be thin and came back up the drain in several slices.

Claude's brother practised flying off the battlements. At first he tried jumping the same way as the wind blew. He flew very fast but it was hard to get back on to the castle roof. Then he tried jumping in the other direction. He flew a very short way before the wind blew him back. Sometimes he wasn't sure where he was because he got mixed up with the smoke from the kitchen fire.

Annabelle was bored. She decided to go down to the dungeons. There were a lot of old things down there which might be interesting. She put on lots of sweaters to keep warm. In her pocket she carried a torch, a plastic bag and a piece of cake.

Last year Mr King had put up a light in the dungeon. Annabelle could see all around except for in the corners. She was glad she had brought her torch. There was nothing in the middle of the dungeon. All the interesting things were in the corners. In one corner she found a mouse nest with three babies in it. She gave them some cake crumbs. In the next was an old coat which fell to dust when she tried to pick it up. In the third corner was a heap of chains, which she put in her plastic bag for Claude and his brother. In the last corner was a trap door.

The trap door lid was heavy. It took Annabelle a long time to open it.

Inside it was black velvet dark. There was a cobwebby ladder leading from the trap door, down into another deep dungeon.

Annabelle climbed down and shone her torch. There was a smell of dust and earth and damp.

Right over the other side of the deep, deep dungeon was what looked like a heap of bones. Annabelle shone her torch at the bones.

It wasn't just a heap of bones. It was a proper skeleton, sitting against the wall.

"Oh, you poor thing," said Annabelle. "You must be cold sitting here."

The skeleton didn't answer. It was too stiff to say anything.

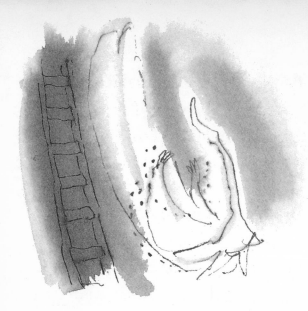

Claude was tired of climbing up through drains. He decided to have a short rest in the dungeon while he was down there.

He saw the trap door. It was still open. Claude liked deep, dark places. He floated down the staircase.

"That's a nice skeleton," he said to Annabelle. "Whose is it?"

"It didn't say," said Annabelle. "It's a real one, not a ghost. I'm taking it upstairs."

"It will make a nice ornament," said Claude.

Annabelle wrapped the skeleton up in one of her sweaters. She carried it up the deep, deep dungeon ladder, and then up the other dungeon staircase. Claude stayed behind to tidy up. He could see some rubbish underneath where the skeleton had been.

But it wasn't rubbish. It was an old book with writing in it. Claude whisked over the pages with his wispy fingers. It was a diary.

"I've heard all this before," he muttered. He read some more. "I know all this," he said. He went back to the beginning. "I know why I've seen this before," he said. "It's *my* diary! I wrote it in this very dungeon, three hundred years ago." He was very excited. The skeleton must be his, then!

He floated up the ladder and through the
dungeon. He saw Annabelle showing the
skeleton to Mr and Mrs King.

Mr King admired the skeleton. "It must be
hundreds of years old," he said. "I wonder
who he was?"

Claude was bursting to tell Annabelle
about the diary. He opened his pale mouth to
tell her, but Mrs King said, "Poor chap. We
ought to bury him."

"Why?" said Annabelle.

"He won't rest if he's still above ground," explained Mrs King.

"I wasn't above ground!" said Claude. "I was in the deepest dungeon."

But Mrs King wasn't listening. "The poor chap will be able to rest in his grave if we bury him," she said.

Rest! Claude thought this sounded like a very good idea. He wouldn't have to howl along the heights any more. He wouldn't have to rattle chains along the top corridor.

He would never have to haunt anywhere again.

He tried to tug at Annabelle's arm, but his ghostly fingers slid right through her. He wailed, "Come and see my diary!" but at that very moment his brother screamed happily from the topmost tower.

Claude stopped to think.

If they buried him, he wouldn't be able to play haunting games with his brother.

He wouldn't be able to frighten Mr King in the shaving mirror.

He wouldn't be able to make the visitors jump.

There would be no more Hallowe'en parties with Annabelle and her friends.

"Excuse me," said Claude. "It's me." He pointed to the skeleton.

"Oh, poor Claude!" said Annabelle. "We'll bury you straight away. I shouldn't have moved you."

"We'll carve you a very fine headstone," said Mr King.

"And I'll plant flowers all over your grave," said Mrs King.

"NO!" screamed Claude. He rushed down to the deepest dungeon and whirled round and round the damp walls. He was so upset that sparks fizzed all over him. The diary flew about in the wind, and then caught fire from the sparks. It burned to a cinder.

His brother heard the noise and came down through seven floors to see what was the matter.

Claude told him about Annabelle finding his skeleton, and wanting to bury him so he could rest. Then, together, Claude and his brother went to find the Kings and *made* them listen.

"I don't want to be buried," Claude explained. "I like it here. Couldn't you put my skeleton in a glass case, and show the visitors? Then on special days I could put my skeleton inside me and do a special haunt."

So that is what they did.

Now when you visit Annabelle's castle you will see the skeleton in its glass case.

But only you will know it belongs to Claude.

The End